Not On My Watch

by Brittany Canasi

Rourke
Educational Media
rourkeeducationalmedia.com

www.rourkeeducationalmedia.com

Edited by: Keli Sipperley
Cover layout by: Rhea Magaro
Interior layout by: Jen Thomas
Cover Illustration by: Luca Maggi

Library of Congress PCN Data

Not On My Watch / Brittany Canasi
(History Files)
ISBN (hard cover)(alk. paper) 978-1-68191-672-9
ISBN (soft cover) 978-1-68191-773-3
ISBN (e-Book) 978-1-68191-873-0
Library of Congress Control Number: 2016932445

Printed in the United States of America,
North Mankato, Minnesota

Dear Parents and Teachers,

The History Files series takes readers into significant eras in United States history, allowing them to walk in the shoes of characters living in the periods they've learned about in the classroom. From the journey to a new beginning on the Mayflower, to the strife of the Vietnam War and beyond, each title in this series delves into the experiences of diverse characters struggling with the conflicts of their time.

Each book includes a comprehensive summary of the era, along with background information on the real people that the fictional characters mention or encounter in the novel. Additional websites to visit and an interview with the author are also included.

In addition, each title is supplemented with online teacher/parent notes with ideas for incorporating the book into a lesson plan. These notes include subject matter, background information, inspiration for maker space activities, comprehension questions, and additional online resources. Notes are available at: www.RourkeEducationalMedia.com.

We hope you enjoy the History Files books as much as we do.

Happy reading,
Rourke Educational Media

American School of Bombay
Guided Reading - Grade 4

Table of Contents

Chapter One

"Hope Richardson, pay attention. I'm not here for my health," the woman said.

Hope's governess, Hester Price, stared at her with a look of impatience and annoyance. Today she was to learn the art of conversation, and she frankly couldn't care less about any of it.

"The point of today's lesson is so that when your husband brings over his colleagues, or potential business contacts, you are able to entertain them with grace and eloquence."

Hope looked away so that Hester wouldn't see her roll her eyes.

"And if I wanted to entertain my own business contacts?" Hope asked.

"Don't be ridiculous," Hester said. "A woman's place is in the home and in support of her husband. Women work because their families are poor and because they have no choice. You, my dear, have been born into privilege, and one day you'll marry into privilege."

Hope shook her head and sighed. "Will I be allowed visitors in my prison of privilege?"

"I see we're getting nowhere today. Very well then," Hester said. She rose from the plush armchair she'd placed in front of Hope and dusted off her skirt. "Your father asked that I take you by his work after your lessons. Gather your things, and we can head off."

A wide, brilliant smile came across Hope's face. Going to her father's watch factory was one of her most favorite things. She'd sit in his office and listen in on his meetings, talking with watch dealers or someone trying to sell him the latest and greatest in machinery that'd "revolutionize the watchmaking process," or so they'd say. And when it was time to go over the ledgers, deal with payroll, or review the weekly reports, he'd always involve her, teaching her everything there was to know about running a factory. It made her feel alive.

Hope ran through the second floor of the brownstone she and her father shared in downtown New York, collecting her belongings as she went.

"Honestly, Hope. You mustn't run. Children run. Ladies stroll."

"Well, then teach me how to stroll at that pace, and I'll stroll," she said.

Hester, well-meaning clod that she was, had been hired by her father shortly after Hope's mother passed away six years ago. As a maternal figure, she was laughable. As an educator, she was adequate—that is, if Hope was ever interested in what she was teaching.

Hope and her governess walked along the streets of downtown, passing by the other brownstones that made up her neighborhood. They eventually led to large, cube-like buildings that had a lot less character on the outside. And though they didn't look nearly as vibrant on the outside, Hope knew that they were teeming with life and activity on the inside.

They were factories, and to her, they were their own kind of beautiful.

They walked up to a building that was somewhere in the middle in terms of size. They walked through the front doors of Richardson Timepieces and Hester put her hand on Hope's back.

"Go straight to your father's office, and please try to practice some of what we learned today. Eloquence. The art of conversation."

Not wanting to argue in the lobby of her father's factory, Hope held back the eye roll that was threatening.

"Of course. Have a good day, Hester," she said as she ran up the stairs toward her father's office.

Patrick Richardson, owner and founder of Richardson Timepieces was a tall, broad man who spoke at only one volume: loud. Hope always found it to be warm and familiar. Many people found it to be intimidating and aggressive. So when Hope rounded the hallway to his office, she knew right away that he wasn't in.

She passed through the door of his office and found that it was indeed empty. Making herself comfortable at his desk, she looked through ledgers and documents that lay about his desk.

She looked at some of the shelved books across the room. Finance. Law. History of watchmaking. She took down the history book and idly thumbed through the pages, passing by illustrations of sundials, hourglasses, and pendulums.

After about an hour, she was starting to get bored sitting alone in the room for so long. Looking over at the door to his office, she wondered how much her father would mind if she decided to take a walk around without him. He usually did his walkthroughs with her in the afternoon, and she knew the factory as if she lived there.

It would be fine.

She walked through the hallway that housed her father's office, down the set of stairs at the end, and into the open space that held the factory. The sounds of buzzing, clinking, and hissing of the machines filled her ears. She walked through the aisles in between the machinery, watching men guide machines to cut out small pieces of metal that would make the insides of the timepieces. A man wiped the sweat from his brow on the right, another rolled his sleeves up to his elbows on the left. The factory was much like a Richardson watch itself, with so many moving pieces working together to make something magical.

She rounded a corner and found a young man with dusty blonde hair she didn't recognize reaching inside one of the machines, seemingly trying to fix it.

She stopped walking and watched him. He couldn't have been too much younger than her, maybe a couple of years, but he looked like he was perfectly at home in a factory, as if he'd been working in one for years.

The boy reached up a bit further into the

machine, twisted something, and appeared satisfied with the result. He pulled his hand out of the machine and stood straight, catching Hope's eye.

"Can I help you, Miss?" he said, wiping his hand on a rag that he'd pulled from his back pocket.

Hope gave him a friendly smile. "Just taking a walk around. I haven't noticed you here before. I'm Hope, by the way. Pleased to meet you."

"Name's Joe. Joe Gilbert. I'm new. Used to work at the steel mill just down the road, but I got me a much better deal here now."

"Gilbert!" yelled a voice from down the walkway. A short, portly man with a shiny red face came hobbling down the aisle, a stack of papers hugged tightly into his stomach.

"Well, I think you went and got me in trouble, Miss. You'd better get goin' before Mr. Peters gets a hold of you," Joe said.

"Oh, Tom?" Hope said with a laugh. "He's harmless. Just grumpy as ever."

"Not so sure about that," he said quietly.

"Miss Richardson, I believe your father was looking for you. You'd do well to join him in his office, if you'd please," Tom said as he approached the two of them.

"And you," Tom continued, facing Joe. "You'd do well to remember your place. Miss Richardson is the daughter of Patrick Richardson."

"It was entirely my fault, Tom," she said, her eyes shifting toward Joe. Joe's eyes looked at her in surprise, and she realized it was because she hadn't told him her last name. Apparently leaving out the fact that your father owned the factory was a pretty large detail to forget when introducing yourself.

"Joe, it was nice meeting you. Hope to see you around, then," she said.

Joe dipped his chin in acknowledgment, and Hope gave him one last friendly smile before turning on her heel.

Chapter Two

Hope sat at the long dining table as she waited for her father to come down. They'd come home from the factory about an hour ago, and Hope was absolutely starving.

"Father! Let's eat!" she yelled from the table.

Muffled footsteps came from upstairs and grew louder as they clomped down the stairs and toward the dining room.

"Well I see the money I pay to Miss Price is going to good use. Did she teach you to yell like that?" her father chided.

"I'm an incurable case," she said.

"That's my girl," her father said, amusement evident in his smile.

Gertie, their housekeeper and cook, brought in a tray containing a roast with potatoes surrounding the edges. Hope nearly wept with joy at the smell of it.

"I'll bring the bread out right away, my dears. Just give me one moment," she said.

"Thank you, Gertie," her father said.

Gertrude nodded her head as she walked back toward the kitchen, and her father turned his attention back to Hope.

"So I heard you had a nice walk around the factory today," he said.

"I just really like watching the factory in motion. I waited a bit for you, but when you were still stuck in your meeting, I … explored a bit."

"I'm not cross, you know," he said, cutting into the roast and carving a piece from the side. He placed the cut of meat on Hope's plate and followed with another, then serving himself more than a healthy share of the roast and potatoes.

"You're not?"

"No, I'm not. You're not a child. You're not going to hurt yourself wandering into a machine. And it makes me very proud that you have a natural curiosity for what goes on in my factory."

Hope looked at her father in surprise. She'd just spent the better part of her day learning the idea that women had one job in the world, and that was to serve their husbands.

"My factory wasn't just a business venture for me," he continued. "Watches, and the ability to tell time, have a great deal of importance in the world."

Hope smiled at her father as he began the story she'd heard so many times over the years. But the gleam in her father's eyes as he told the story made her never want to interrupt him.

"In order for a train to make it safely from one city to another, telling time accurately is vital. If a train needs to take one track, they do it on a schedule. Otherwise, you have two trains on the same track, and you can guess how that'd end."

"I think I know how that ends."

"And when Lincoln finished the Gettysburg Address, what did he receive as a gift? A pocket watch!" her father said, throwing his arms up in the air. "Had we been as big as we are now, it could have been a Richardson watch! Lincoln could have been wearing one of my pieces. But regardless, dear daughter, the man was given a pocket watch. It's a very important gift."

He stabbed the meat on his plate with a fork and sawed off a large slice of beef, popping the entire piece in his mouth.

Chewing his food, he sat back in his seat and folded his hands over his belly.

"So, my dear Hope," he said, not fully done chewing, "what did you learn from your walk today?"

Hope tilted her head and thought back to her afternoon at the factory. She thought of Joe, a boy who was young enough to be in school.

"Father, how long have you been employing younger people at the factory?"

Patrick looked over at his daughter, tilting his head curiously as he thought about her question.

"What do you mean by young? Young men? I'd say that's the norm."

"No, young as in younger than me. I noticed there was a boy there today, and he looked like he may be younger than me, though I didn't catch his age."

Her father nodded, chewing another bite of food in a way that looked like he was also chewing on her question.

He took a long, leisurely drink of wine from the glass on the table before sitting back and looking at Hope.

"It's actually fairly normal for younger people to be working, though I'd draw the line somewhere around your age. Many families can't afford to have their sons or daughters not work when they get to a certain age. Very sad indeed, but I let Tom deal with the employees and I try not to think on it too much."

"Think on what?" Hope asked.

"The fact that life doesn't always work out for people as we'd like, and that sometimes we're the cause of it."

Hope looked at her father in disbelief. It was the first time she'd heard her father speak about his work in a way that didn't bring him the utmost pride.

She wondered why he continued to run his factory in a way that made him feel that way, but she could tell that it probably wasn't the best time to push on the subject.

"Anyhow," he said, serving himself a piece of fresh bread from the basket Gertie had brought out, as well as another slice of roast, "it's nothing you need to concern yourself with, either. Your job is to learn the art of running a business and oversee those who oversee for you, just as I do."

Hope smiled at her father and nodded. She was glad her father supported her interest in the factory and excited for the next time she'd be there, but his words from earlier still lingered in her mind. Young people. Forced to work. And he'd said he drew the line at a certain age. But did others?

Chapter Three

Hope returned to the factory a couple of days later, newly reassured by her father that she could, and should, take a more active role in the factory. He was in a meeting with a man she didn't recognize, and it was taking a lot longer than she'd thought. So partly to kill time and partly to continue learning the ins and outs of the place, she took another walk.

She went along the narrow walkways in between machines, and she stopped by one of the large cutters. A tall, lanky man monitored the machine as it did its work.

"Hi there," she said, smiling at the man as he looked up from the machine.

The man smiled at her, but his eyes were wary. "Hello, Miss. What can I help you with?"

"What does this machine do?" she asked.

"It cuts the pieces that go inside the watch.

See these guys?" he said, holding up very tiny circles that had ridges along the edges. "They all move together to make the watch work. We make a bunch of 'em at once, and they can go inside any watch."

Hope's eyes glowed. She was fascinated. "That's wonderful. And you put them together when they're done?"

The man laughed, the sound smoky and rusty as if he didn't do it often enough. "Gosh no. I have one job, and it's to make these pieces. Someone else puts them together, but I honestly have no idea who does. They just collect the pieces and take 'em away."

Hope nodded, thanking the man for showing her how the machine worked. She waved as she continued down the walkway. Some machines cut the small wheel-like pieces, some cut what looked like watch faces, and some did things that were a complete mystery to her. It was genius how the work was set up. Everyone had one single job.

"Another pay cut?" she heard to her right.

"… extended the hours. Working more for less."

"This is absurd."

Hope hid behind an unoccupied machine, peeking around to see who was speaking. Two men, shorter and stockier than the man she'd been talking to earlier, were huddled closely, one of them leaning against a support beam that came down from the ceiling.

"…treating us like animals…"

"…barely feed my family as it is…"

The buzzing of the factory in combination with others talking around her made it increasingly difficult to hear the men. She leaned her head closer to hear better, but she could only hear bits and pieces. However, the point of the conversation was pretty clear. They weren't happy, and it sounded like they had a good reason.

"… don't pay like they used to," she overheard from the one leaning against the pole.

"Hey, you supposed to be here?" said a

woman's voice behind her.

Hope startled as she about-faced and looked in the direction of the woman.

"Sorry, I was, I was just resting for a moment," she lied. "I'll—I'll just be going."

Hope ducked her head and walked away before the woman could ask too many questions. She wanted to hear more of what the men were saying or if they intended to do anything, but the last thing she needed was for people to find out the owner's daughter was eavesdropping on the workers.

She weaved in and out of the walkways between machines, looking for one person in particular.

"Good afternoon, Joe," she said from a distance. Joe had his hand deep inside a machine, and she guessed it probably wasn't a good idea to startle him.

He made a few clinking noises inside the machine, tapped the top of it as a manner of finality, and stepped down to Hope's level.

"Hello, Miss Hope," he said.

"Please, just call me Hope," she said.

"Probably shouldn't, Miss. Ain't right. Ain't my place and all."

Hope huffed out a breath and looked at the ceiling. Looked like Tom had given him a talking to, and now they were stuck in an awkward dance of formality.

Joe grabbed one of the two rags hanging from his back pocket and wiped some grease marks off of the machine.

"What is your job here?" she asked.

"You asking as my boss's daughter, or you asking just regular?"

"Just regular, I suppose," she said. He seemed wary of her. Suspicious even.

"Well then in that case, I fix the machines," he said, setting his shoulders back with pride.

"All by yourself?" she asked. "That's pretty impressive."

Joe raised an eyebrow in question. "How old do you think I am?"

"I suppose—" she said, drawing out the last word, "ten or eleven?"

"I'm fourteen."

Hope's eyes widened in shock, and she studied him up and down, trying to make sense of this. His shoes looked much too small to belong to someone her age, and his height wasn't close, either. But his small, pale face did look a bit older, now that she looked closer, and his caramel eyes seemed to have a little more skepticism than a ten year old's should have.

"I know what you're thinkin'," he said, moving his head so that he was in her line of sight. "Ma and Pop were fresh off the boat from Ireland when I was born," he said. "Didn't have a whole lot of food growing up, they say that's why I'm smaller than I should be."

"That's absolutely awful," she said. "I'm so sorry you went through that."

Hope imagined a baby Joe, crying in his crib—if he even had one—and not knowing why no one was feeding him. Or being the mother or father who had to helplessly look on as their child went to bed hungry once again. It was heartbreaking.

"I ain't trying to make you feel sorry for me, Miss Hope. I'm just trying to explain why I'm short is all. We do just fine now. Pop's got a big, round belly, and we haven't gone to bed hungry in years. Havin' me work helps 'em too, so I don't mind it at all."

Hope nodded, telling herself to bury the pity and let it go.

"How long have you worked in factories?" she asked.

"About four years. Before that I sold papers, did odd jobs here and there. Whatever folks would pay me for."

"But, you never went to school?" she said, her tone underlined with more surprise than she meant.

"Don't have a whole lot of use for school. Just gotta know how to work now, don't I? They don't need me to learn how watches were invented. They just want me to fix the machines that make 'em."

Joe smiled at her, making sure she knew that he'd been joking.

"Well, I gotta get back to this before Mr. Peters comes by and gives me another talkin' to," he said.

"Of course," she said. "I didn't mean to hold you up." She turned on her heel to walk away.

"Why don't you come back and visit?" he said. "You can tell me about your fancy life, and I can tell you what it's like to work in places like this. Job gets a little lonely sometimes. Could be nice to have a friend every once in a while. If you're fine with that, of course," he said bashfully.

"I'd love that! I'll be back in a day or so," Hope said excitedly, leaving him to his work.

For the next two weeks, she visited him a few times a week. She kept him entertained as he did his sometimes-monotonous work, trading stories of factory life and funny stories from Hester's failed attempts to make her a lady. They enjoyed each other's company immensely.

Neither realized the whispers of turmoil in the factory had grown louder around them.

Chapter Four

Hope sat in her father's study as she waited for him to come home from the factory. A needlepoint hoop lay in her lap, barely begun. Hester had taught her how to embroider that afternoon, and her assignment was to embroider a rose before the next day's lesson.

"Think of the beautiful pillows and cushions you could create for your home!" Hester effused. Hope had wanted to laugh at how ridiculous she sounded, but she was raised better than that. So she'd disguised her amusement in a rather large smile.

"Yes, I should have more pillows than I could ever need. Or want," Hope said. And then she promptly changed the subject to when they'd be able to stop by the factory.

"I was given strict instructions to not

bring you by today," said Hester, her nose turned up to brook no further argument.

So now Hope sat in the empty room, the large grandfather clock reminding her of the passing time with each tick, tock, or bell chime. What could her father have possibly wanted to keep from her? She was always welcome at the factory, whether it was to sit with him or explore on her own.

"Hope!"

Gertie's voice carried from the bottom of the stairs, making its muffled way into the study.

Hope flung the needlepoint onto the couch. Maybe she could just draw a rose on the fabric and consider it done. Maybe she could just tell Hester that, much like entertaining her future husband's business associates, she wasn't cut out for embroidery.

She opened the door to the study and stood near the top of the stairs, looking over the railing at Gertie.

"Dear, dinner is ready. Come on down

before it gets cold."

"Where's my father?" Hope asked.

"I haven't the slightest, but let's not wait any longer for dinner. It's getting late."

Hope's shoulders slumped as she dragged her feet down the stairs. She couldn't remember the last time her father hadn't made it home for dinner. Since her mother had passed away, he said it was his top priority to make sure that she never ate alone. The anxiousness that had begun during her lesson was starting to intensify, and her appetite withered.

When she got to the bottom of the stairs, Gertie gently patted her on the back.

"Don't you worry, dear."

Hope nodded her head and smiled, though it felt like a loose-fitting bandage.

She sat at the table, fiddled around with the chicken and roasted vegetables on her plate, cutting pieces and shuffling them around, and decided long after the food had gone cold that she wasn't hungry.

And her father still hadn't come home.

She looked out the window of the dining room, the streets below almost completely dark, the occasional hoof beats of carriages passing by.

"Hope, you should eat something," Gertie said from the doorway to the dining room. "I'm going to turn in after dinner, and there won't be anything for you to eat until morning."

"Sorry, Gertie. Of course, I'm just a little distracted is all."

"He's just held up at work, dear. He'll be home soon enough. Now eat before your food gets cold," the woman said, giving Hope a warm smile before walking out of sight.

Hope picked at the chicken and ate just enough to where she wouldn't be hungry, and pinched a roasted carrot between her fingers and brought it to her mouth.

"Good enough," she said to no one, pushing in her chair and going to her room.

Feeling more tired than usual, likely from

her nerves being on edge for most of the day, Hope readied herself for bed. If time wasn't passing while she was awake, then it would surely pass while she was sleeping.

Hope laid in bed, tossing and turning, and tossing and turning some more. But sleep was no closer to coming than it had been when she first attempted it.

A door opened down the hallway.

Her father was finally home.

She jumped out of bed and tiptoed down the hallway, wanting to see what he was up to. Peering into the doorway, she found her father at his desk with his head in his hands, barely moving a muscle.

"Father?" she said quietly.

Her father slowly lifted his head from his hands, and even in the dim light of the lamps, she could see the look on his face. He looked exhausted, and worse, he looked … defeated?

"Hello sunshine," he said. The corners of his mouth turned up in a weak attempt at a smile. His voice was eerily muted, a stark departure from its usual loud, emphatic volume.

Hope walked into the office, concern etched in her face.

"Are you—are you okay?"

"Oh, sure," he said. "Just a very busy day at the factory, that's all."

Hope didn't believe it. Not for one second.

"Are you sure?"

Her father sighed, looked up at the ceiling, and then put his head back in his hands.

"The workers went on strike. Half of them are gone. I—I'm ruined, Hope."

Hope's stomach sank. She thought back to the men she overheard in the factory.

Barely able to feed their families. Feeling like they were being treated like animals. More pay cuts. It was all leading up to this. And she, well, she knew about it and said nothing. Now her father's factory was about to go under because of it.

"Father," she said, steeling herself for what she was about to say. "I overheard the men talking about it."

"Talking about it when?" her father said, raising his head from his hands to look at her.

"When I was walking around the factory a couple of weeks ago. They seemed upset."

"Oh, don't pay any mind to that. It was common knowledge that the workers were upset. That's no surprise at all."

Hope looked at him in confusion. "But if you knew that they were unhappy—"

"The surprise wasn't that they were unhappy. That we all knew. The surprise was that they weren't willing to wait just a little longer for me to figure out a solution. Instead, they walked out today. Sure, some stayed. But not enough," he said.

"So what will you do?" Hope asked quietly.

"Not the faintest idea," her father said, his voice full of despair. "It's now up to Tom. I told him to come up with a solution while I try to negotiate with the workers."

She walked over to him and gave him a hug, but he didn't move to return it. He only sat at his desk, tense and distant.

"How can I help?" Hope asked. She knew in reality there was little she could do, but it still felt better to at least offer. At least show her father she wanted to do something and not feel so powerless in this situation.

"You can stay out of the way during this."

Hope pulled back and stood before him. Stay out of it? What good was that possibly going to do, to just leave her father when he was in what would probably be the biggest professional dilemma of his life? How was that supposed to be helping?

"Stay … out of it?" she asked, trying to understand the words as they left her mouth.

"Yes, the factory is no place for you right now."

"Father, they're upset workers, not violent criminals."

"I just can't have any distractions right now," he snapped. He looked out the window as he said the words, as if saying them without looking her in the eyes made them somehow sting less.

It didn't.

So that's the reason why she should stay home. Because she was a distraction. As a woman was.

"I see," she said. She backed away from his desk and walked to the door.

"I'll just be heading to bed, then. Don't want to distract you any longer."

"Hope, wait one moment," her father said, finally attempting to make eye contact.

"No, Father. I think I'll go to sleep."

Hope walked quickly back to her room before her father could call out for her.

She laid in bed and stared up at the ceiling. So her father's factory was in jeopardy, and he saw her as little more than a distraction. The former was awful, and her heart ached for the amount of stress he was under. Hope had no idea what it was like to toil for something for so long, to grow it from infancy, and then to have it ripped from beneath you.

But the latter, the feeling of being nothing

more than a bother, well, that was just awful. And it hurt. She expected that kind of talk from Hester, who essentially said her entire existence was so that her future husband was happy. To hear her father essentially validate every word that came from her mouth was a punch to the stomach. It meant that Hester didn't say those words because she personally thought it was true.

She said them because Patrick Richardson did, too.

Chapter Five

Hope sat through one of the longest, most boring lessons in recent history. Hester was trying her hardest to teach her French, and Hope had barely listened to a word of it. After hour four of trying to teach Hope how to say, "Would you like some tea?" and "Please join us in the parlor," Hester had given up and left for the day.

Finally alone, Hope snuck out of the house and to the factory, despite her father's edict. She made her way there in less than half the usual time, her breath heavy from the exertion. When she arrived, she was startled by what she found.

There were men yelling, chanting together, and shaking their fists in the air.

"Fair pay for fair work!"

"We have needs, you have greed!"

Some just stood with their arms crossed over their chest, looking angry and shaking with rage.

It looked like little had improved over the past couple of weeks.

Hope decided it'd be a bad idea to walk through the crowd of men, so she walked past the factory, praying they'd just think her another curious passerby. Once she reached the corner, she rounded the building to the back and entered through a service door she'd seen a few times. The door was used often by the workers, so it was unlocked.

The service door opened up to the factory floor, which was still buzzing, but at a noticeably quieter volume. For every two men that used to work in the factory, there was now only one. And the occasional chat in the middle of the walkways was a thing of the past. Everyone seemed on edge. Afraid, even.

Hope walked up and down the aisles of the factory, looking for Joe. Would he even be here? Or would he be outside with the other strikers? She hadn't recognized him from the street, but she was too afraid to get close enough to really see.

As she rounded a corner, that's when she noticed the biggest difference of all.

There were a lot less grown men and women in the factory, and a lot more people that looked like Joe.

And then she saw him. He didn't have his usual two grease rags hanging out of his back pockets, body hunched over a machine, trying to figure out what made it work— or not work. No, now he stood up straight, proud even, and watched over one of the young boys as he did the same job Joe usually did.

She watched as he pointed to different parts of the machine, say a few words, and then the boy would move to that part of the machine, studying it and tinkering with his tools.

Hope rushed over to him, grateful to see a familiar face.

"Joe!" she said breathlessly. "Joe, what's

happening here? Everyone's so angry outside, and it's been two weeks. Why hasn't anything changed?"

Joe looked over at her, surprise evident in his eyes.

"Can you keep your voice down?" he hissed. He held up a finger to the boy he was helping.

"Be back in a minute, Jimmy. Keep adjustin' the wheel on that one."

Joe walked away and stopped about ten yards away from where the boy was working.

"You can't just come in here and start askin' questions about the strike like that," he said in a hushed tone. He looked over his shoulder, and then the other, as if he expected someone to be listening in. "We've been barred from mentioning it. They say we'll get the boot on the spot if they catch wind of it."

"Why?" Hope said. "Who is 'they'? Who is saying that?"

"Well, Tom really. But he said the order came from above. Don't know if I believe him, but I also know I ain't really in a position to lose my job right now."

"No, no of course not. But Joe, why are there so many more young people working here? Is that how they're trying to replace the workers on strike?"

"Yeah, they say we're—er, younger people— are less likely to strike, easier to pay a low wage and make 'em work longer hours. He looked over his shoulders again, breathing in a sigh of relief when he saw that they were still alone.

"They used to work in the assembly room before," he said. "It's a room in the back where they put the pieces together. But they've been moved up since, and I'm supposed to be supervising them."

Hope nodded. "So who works in the assembly room now?"

"Dunno. I just know that they told me one day that I was in charge of these guys, and they'd give me a couple extra dollars a week for it. Can't say that I hate the extra money, though I feel awful that so many men are gettin' a raw deal out of it."

"Well, that's good news for you, Joe. I just … I just hate that it's come to this. That they'd rather hire children instead of talk things out with all these men who are upset."

"Hope, you need to be careful. There's somethin' goin' on. I don't know what it is, but it's been strange around here, and I've had a bad feeling for a while. I've been keepin' my head down and trying to go about my business. But it isn't good. You look after yourself. Maybe go home, I dunno. Don't think this is the place for you right now."

Hope stared at Joe in disbelief. She expected it from Hester, and she'd accepted the fact that her father also felt the same, and now Joe.

"Where should I be, Joe? At home learning how to be a proper little rich girl?" she asked.

"Well, kind of. No — wait. That's not how I meant it—"

"It's fine, Joe. I know exactly how you meant it. Congratulations again on the promotion, truly. I'll see you around." She turned on her heel and swiftly walked away.

"Hope," he said somewhat impatiently. It made her feel like a petulant child, which only made her madder.

He called her name twice more, and she ignored those as well, feeling her face heat in anger and hurt. She felt embarrassed and silly, and was starting to believe that she didn't belong there. Like she belonged, well, home. Learning French. Learning to carry a light but slightly educational conversation for the sake of a man.

So she walked toward the exit, deciding that they had won. She wouldn't come back.

She walked past rows of younger boys operating machines, a few women here and there, and even fewer men interspersed among the factory. The mood of the factory was well matched with her own. It was bleak.

As she neared the exit, she noticed a door to her left that she'd ignored on her way in. It usually was closed, so she'd never paid much attention to it, but now it was open just a crack, a sliver of light leaking through the side.

Hope looked behind her to see if anyone was nearby, and she found herself alone. She quietly walked to the open door, trying to not let the soles of her shoes make too much noise against the stone floor. She peeked inside the crack, and what she saw inside had her blood running cold.

The room was mostly silent, save for an occasional giggle or a tiny cough. Lots of tiny coughs. Unlike the factory, warmed by the engines of several machines, the draft coming from the room was ice cold.

And the room was full of small children assembling watches.

Some of them looked to be a couple years younger than Joe. Others looked like they were barely older than five.

They worked small, grimy fingers as they sorted pieces and assembled the watches. Hope opened the door wider, its hinges giving a protesting squeak as if it was warning her that she didn't belong there.

Well, she didn't belong in the factory at all, so what difference did it make? She walked into the room, knowing she wasn't going to like anything else she found.

She walked up to a little boy who looked to be one of the youngest.

"Hello, there," she said.

The little boy looked up, his white fingers cold from the frigid room temperature were covered in grey dirt and grease from the metal pieces. He had been sorting watch parts into different boxes, and he'd done such a good job at it. Tears pricked the corners of Hope's eyes.

"Hiya, Miss," the tiny voice said. He was missing a front tooth, and his smile was silly and sweet.

"How long have you worked here?" she asked.

"Dunno," he said, lifting his shoulders for added effect.

"We all been here since last Tuesday," a girl said from down the table. She looked to be a couple of years older than the boy.

"How old are you?" she asked the boy.

"I'm five!" he said with great pride.

Her heart sank to her stomach as a cold, lifeless lump. Her guess had been right, and the validation felt more awful than she could've imagined. The boy's eyes blinked sharply as he looked at Hope, probably wondering what she was doing there.

"Why did you come work here?" she asked.

"My momma just said I hads to. I dunno. But they keep it real cold in here. Miss Lady, do you think there's a way to make it not cold?"

She heard a quiet din of agreement from the room, and she felt like she was going to be sick. All around the room were similar small faces, pale but flushed from the cold, dirt and grease smeared on their faces, their clothes in varying levels of disrepair.

"I'll … I'll see what I can do. What's your name, sweetheart?" she asked the boy.

"Ben, Miss Lady. But Momma calls me Benjamin when she's real mad."

Hope gave the young boy a smile, her eyelids threatening to release a tear from her glassy eyes.

"Well it's very lovely to meet you, Ben. And since I'm not angry, I'll just call you that. How about that?"

Ben rewarded her with another of his gap-toothed smiles, and Hope put a hand on his shoulder, giving it a reassuring squeeze. She looked around the room once more, her heart in a million pieces.

Her father may not think she had any business here, and maybe Joe didn't think so either, but she'd never felt more that she was right where she needed to be. Because the strike was one thing, and she wasn't really sure what she could do to help end it. But this, the use of small, young children to create something that was just getting sold for a profit, was wrong. They belonged in school. They belonged running in a park, playing a made up game until the sun went down. They did not belong toiling away in a windowless, freezing room.

She wondered if her father knew about this. She knew he took an active hand in the finances of the factory, but he seldom knew the small details of how things ran. Just that they did.

She left the room quietly, determined to march into his office and drag him down to the assembly room.

"Where do you think you're going?" came a low, gravelly voice.

Hope startled, her head jerking to the right to see where the voice was coming from, though she already knew who it belonged to.

Tom stood about five feet away, his feet set wide and his hands on his hips. He looked even more menacing than usual, his greasy eyelids squinting at her as if he were issuing a challenge. Hope stood up straighter and pushed her shoulders back.

"I'm going to see my father, not that it's any of your concern, Tom."

"I believe you mean Mr. Peters."

"No, I think I'll stay with Tom. As respect is earned, and by the looks of things, you haven't earned much," she said, throwing away any semblance of manners she'd been taught.

"And what do you need your father for?" he said, moving closer.

Warning bells went off in Hope's head, and her stomach grew acidic with nerves.

"I think we both know the answer, so please get out of my way."

She moved forward to walk around him when he grabbed her left shoulder with an amount of force that terrified Hope, the knuckles of his fat fingers turning white from the strength of his grip.

"Get your filthy hand off of me, or I'll scream so loud your ears will bleed."

"Let me just remind you of one thing, and

then you're free to do as you please, Hope," he said, spitting out her name in a hiss.

Hope said nothing in response, only stared straight at him in challenge. To be honest, he terrified her, with the look of pure evil in his eyes and the aura that he really didn't care about anyone or anything. But there was no way she was letting him know that.

He smiled then, his lip flared in a sneer, as if he were enjoying this way too much. He took a step closer to her, and she could smell the acrid scent of sweat and stale beer. She was about to lose her lunch.

"Just remember, your father puts me in charge of this place, and I'll do what I see fit to keep it running. You run your mouth to him about anything you've seen here, anything at all, and your little friend Joe is out of here. I'll make sure he never works in this city again, and I'll probably forget to pay him for the work he's done. So you decide how you want this to end. Sound good, sweetheart?"

Hope stood paralyzed. She could help the

young children in the assembly room, but Joe would lose his job and would likely have trouble finding a new one. She thought back to his story of being a young child without food, and it suddenly made her choice much, much harder.

If she stayed silent, there was no telling how much worse things could get. But what choice did she have? No matter what, lives could be irreparably ruined.

And he knew it. Tom knew the quandary it left her in. He knew he had her.

"That's what I thought," he said with another sneer. "Why don't you scamper on home, sweetheart. This place isn't for a young lady such as yourself."

He kept his grip on her shoulder a beat longer as if in warning, and Hope's stomach roiled with nausea. She slapped his hand away with as much force as she could manage and walked out.

She stopped two feet from the back door and turned to him.

"Watch your back, you piece of garbage. If you think you've won, you're wrong."

Tom's head shot back ever so subtly, clearly surprised at her cheek. He then looked her up and down, found her lacking, and then barked out a laugh.

Hope shook her head and stormed out of the factory. Did she think she could've prevented this? Probably not. But it wouldn't have gone on for two weeks before her father was made aware of it. Tom would have been found out, her father would have put a stop to it, and things would have begun to go back to normal.

When her father came home later tonight, they were having a serious discussion about his tendency to give a morally corrupt man such as Tom free reign over the factory. It was his company, and he needed to see the reality of what happened when a man who cared about no one had power over everyone.

Chapter Six

Her father had skipped dinner again, something that had become a regular occurrence since things took a turn for the worse at the factory. Hope sat in silence, too nervous to do more than nibble on a few bites and push the rest around her plate. And as she walked down the hall to her father's study, her stomach's growl gave away her presence.

Her father sat near the fireplace, the wood recently lit and the room not yet warmed up. The damp coolness in the room made her all the more uncomfortable, giving her even less courage to do what she needed. She closed her eyes for a moment, inhaling a deep, cold breath through her nostrils, and continued forward until she was standing in front of him.

If she did this the right way, she'd be able

to bring to light what was happening at the factory, have Tom fired, and have Joe keep his job. She just needed to find the right words.

"Father, we need to talk."

"Sure, Hope. What is it?" he asked. But he barely looked at her, and his tone sounded like he'd rather be doing anything else than having a conversation.

"We need to talk about what I saw today. Please don't get angry, but I went by the factory."

Her father's face stayed mostly impassive, save for the flare in his eyes that gave away his annoyance.

"Fine. And?"

"And I think you know what I'm about to say. The factory can't go on like it is. There were children there, Father."

"There have always been children there, Hope," he said impatiently. "We've discussed this before. It's a sad reality, and I don't really want to bring it up again. We do what we have to do."

"No, Father. Not just people around my age."

"That's enough!" he bellowed, standing up to his full height.

Hope jumped back, never having heard her father raise his voice to her.

"I have a business to run, and sacrifices are to be made. There are men far wealthier than me who have to make the same choices every day, and they don't have someone lecturing them about it. Rockefeller! Do you think when Rockefeller's workers complained, he bent to their will?"

"That's not the same, I just …"

"He didn't!" her father continued, his eyes wild and full of rage. "He bought every oil refinery in the area. If those workers thought they'd go elsewhere for work, they were wrong. You worked for Rockefeller, or you didn't work at all."

"That's barbaric," she whispered.

"That's life! That's business!"

"This isn't you. This isn't the man I've

known my entire life, whose passion for creating never exceeded his greed for more money," she said, backing away from him and heading toward the door.

"I'm not being greedy, Hope," he said, attempting to reel in his anger. "You don't understand how much cost there is in creating watches. I can't give my workers any more money."

"There has to be a way."

"There isn't. Eighty percent of the cost of making a watch is just in the labor. If I give the workers any more money, I'm barely making a profit. And if I'm not making a profit, the place goes under, and then no one has a job."

Hope stood there, chewing on her lip as she contemplated what he'd said.

"Father," she began calmly, "surely there is another way that you could turn things around. These chil–"

"I don't want to hear another word about it!" he barked. "I told you before that I hired

Tom to make the decisions I don't need to make myself, and the entire reason for that is so that I don't have to hear about it. I give him a problem, he fixes it, and that's all I need to know."

Well, that was that then, Hope thought. Her father's problem wasn't that he couldn't come up with a better solution. It was that he didn't care to.

"Well, if you feel that way, then there's nothing more I can do," she said, turning to walk out of the room.

"And Hope?" he said, his gaze still fixed on the fireplace.

Hope paused and looked over her shoulder, waiting for him to continue.

"You aren't to go back to the factory. I told you once, and I won't tell you again."

"But, Father!"

"Not another word. If I can't keep you out of there with words, I'll keep you away with distance. Your Aunt Muriel will be more than happy for you pay an extended visit."

His tone was harsh, and the threat cut straight through her. Her Aunt Muriel was a bitter, old woman who lived in upstate New York in a small town with little to do. She had lived a lonely life with little else but her spiteful personality to keep her company. The promise of living with Aunt Muriel would be tantamount to a prison sentence.

She said nothing in return as she shook her head and went to her room. Trembling with frustration, anger, and sadness, she closed her door and leaned against it, slowly sinking to the floor. Her relationship with her father had devolved so quickly in such a short amount of time. Now it was like she lived with a stranger. A stranger who was consistently disappointed in her.

Her feelings aside, she needed to focus on what was most important. It wasn't the threat of being sent to live in the middle of nowhere with a miserable aunt. It wasn't lamenting the loss of her relationship with her father. It was saving the childhood of several little people that worked at the factory, and countless others that would work there one day if she stood by and did nothing.

Chapter Seven

It was as if her father had automatically assumed she would disobey him.

Gertie was under strict orders to accompany Hope any time she left the house, and Hester was to report any attempts to leave, or any misbehavior at all, directly to her father.

Never mind having to move to upstate New York with Aunt Muriel. It was as if Hope was already a prisoner.

Hope was going through the motions, feeling like a lifeless scarecrow being pushed through the same actions each day. All while painfully, heartbreakingly aware of what was still going on at the factory. She felt powerless. She felt... like everyone else had won.

Today she was to practice the piano. Hope

looked at the sheet music in front of her, Hester sitting to her left and telling her the progression of the music, when to use the damper pedal by her right foot, and discussed the tempo of the song. Hope only saw each note as someone poking at her, taunting her. *This is your future. You belong here. Stop trying to insert yourself in a man's world. Silly. Silly. Girl.*

The feeling of helplessness made her feel positively sick.

Sick. Wait. Wait just a moment. What if... she somehow wasn't able to have lessons all day? What if she were so sick that she was forced to stay in bed? Nothing serious that'd require a visit from the doctor, just something that would make her ill enough to require bed rest. Surely that would necessitate a day off from lessons and afford her just enough time to slip out undetected for the amount of time it'd take to cover the several blocks between her and Richardson Timepieces.

Hope woke up the next morning with her

theatrics already in play. She had begged off early from dinner the night before, saying she was beginning to feel ill. She gingerly held her throat and blamed it on the change in weather. Just a sore throat, she said. She really hoped she'd feel better in the morning.

"I'm afraid I'm not much better this morning," she said as Gertie came in to check on her. She spoke in her best impression of someone whose sinuses were completely blocked, her voice nasally and pathetic.

"Oh, dear," Gertie said, putting her hand to Hope's forehead. "Well, you don't seem to have a temperature, so I don't think we need to fetch a doctor."

"No, I don't think so either," Hope said, pretending to clear her throat with great effort.

"Perhaps a day or two of rest will do you some good? I'll bring some broth up to you in a bit."

"I think rest sounds lovely."

Gertie nodded and gave Hope a warm smile

as she exited the room. When Hope heard her footsteps reach the stairs, the sounds of footfalls more and more distant, she jumped out of bed and dressed as quickly as she possibly could.

She grabbed the first dress she found in her wardrobe, slipped it on over her underclothes, and fastened it with haste. Her hair was still a mess, sticking out in various directions and a cloud of frizz at the top, but it'd have to stay that way. She could cover her clothes up with the bed sheets, but it was going to be hard to explain why her hair was suddenly coiffed when she was supposed to be bedridden. She donned the first pair of shoes she could find and jumped back into bed, covering herself up to her chin.

A few moments later, Gertie came in with her broth.

"Hester just showed up. I let her know that you would be spending the rest of the day in bed, so she'll be back tomorrow. I hope that's all right, dear."

Relief flooded Hope. So far, everything was working. There was one less person keeping a constant eye on her. Now all she had to do was find her moment to leave the house.

"Would you like me to stay while you finish your broth?" Gertie asked.

"No, thank you," Hope said nervously. If even the slightest detail went wrong in her plan, the entire thing would blow up.

"Now I know that if a doctor were here, he'd say to continue drinking broth, nothing else," Gertie continued. "But I know that when I'm sick, I just want things that are awful for me. Think you could handle it if I baked a pie? Say... cherry pie?"

Hope's eyes widened and her mouth watered, thinking of Gertie baking her favorite pie, when she realized what it meant.

It meant she finally had her chance. Gertie's pies were no small endeavor.

"I–I'd really love that, Gertie. Thank you," she said.

Well, if everything failed and her father forced her to pack her things and move to Aunt Muriel's, at least she'd have a delicious pie to drown her sorrows in at the end of the day.

"You know, my dear," Gertie said as she got up and headed for the door, "don't think I haven't noticed the change in your father since things have happened at the factory."

Hope looked at her in surprise. Gertie had been a part of their family since the very beginning, but her involvement in family affairs was non-existent. She was there as a caretaker and occasionally a friend but never busied herself with anything that would force her to take sides.

"Just know, my dear," she said, "that I'm on your side. And I'll support you in whatever choices you make in life."

Well, then. Side taken.

"Now I'm going to go downstairs, and I'll be down there for about one hour before I have to come up." She had a funny look in her eyes, as if she were trying to push another message into Hope's head. One that she wouldn't dare say out loud.

That's when Hope knew. Gertie knew all along that she'd planned to leave the house. Of course she did; nothing got past the woman who'd known Hope her whole life. And not known her as Hester did, as a mind to be molded, but just as she was.

Hope could barely react to Gertie's words. She sat there in bed, the covers gathered tight under her chin. She nodded ever so slightly, and Gertie smiled at her as she left the room.

It was now or never, though she felt a little silly sneaking out at this point.

She rushed out of bed in a tumble, her messy braid swinging to the front as she righted herself.

Hope glided down the stairs as quietly as she could, realizing halfway down that she was sneaking out from habit. She ran down the street, passing block after block toward the factory. She was no longer in a race against time, but the sense of urgency she felt in what she had to do kept her running at a breakneck pace.

The workers were still picketing outside, though there were fewer, and the crowd was less aggressive.

They were giving up.

She rushed in through the service door, then up and down the aisles of machinery, hiding in between the machines as she heard people coming. And there, hovering over a young boy working on a sewing machine, was Joe.

She looked over her shoulder to make sure no one was coming, then ran over to him as quickly as possible.

"Joe!" she whispered loudly in a hiss. "Joe!"

He whipped around to face Hope, his eyes wide in shock.

"Joe, I need your help, and I need your permission."

Joe's head shot back as he looked at her

with suspicion.

"My permission? Hope, what's goin' on with you?"

"The assembly room—Joe, there are little children in there. Barely older than five or six."

Anger flared in Joe's eyes. He looked at the younger boy working on the sewing machine, held up a hand telling him to wait a moment, and then moved away so that they could speak without being overheard.

"What? How do you know?" he said.

"The last time I was here. They're so young, Joe. We have to do something."

"So what do you need my permission for? Your father owns this place. I'm boss of maybe five people."

"When I first saw them," she said, looking over both shoulders again, "Tom found me. He said that if I told anyone he'd, he'd…"

"He'd what?"

"He'd fire you, leave you without pay, and make sure you never worked in the city again. I don't know if he's able to do that, but I couldn't risk it without telling you first."

Her eyes were pleading, begging him to understand that she knew how difficult this situation was. That it was one thing to be relegated to the middle of nowhere with a miserable aunt, but it was another entirely to have no money for food. The person who'd hurt the most if things went south wasn't her. It was Joe.

Joe's jaw tensed as he ground his teeth together. He looked around the factory, presumably for Tom, anger in his eyes as a vein at his temple throbbed.

"I hate him so much it makes my blood boil," Joe said.

"You and me both," she said, lifting a corner of her mouth in a half-smile.

"So what's your plan?"

"You mean you're fine with it? Are you sure? Joe, this could end really badly."

"Don't care. I wanna help, and I want Tom punished. He's run this place into the ground, and he's ruinin' enough lives already in the process."

Hope smiled in relief and threw herself forward, her arms wrapping around Joe's shoulders.

"You are the best, Joe. Thank you so much for doing this with me."

Joe held his hands out like he wasn't sure what was happening. He slowly brought a hand to Hope's upper back and patted it hesitantly, as if he was burping a baby.

"You're welcome?" he said, standing stiffly. It was as if no one had ever hugged him before.

Hope stood back and bit her lip. "Here's the tricky part. And you may not like this, but I don't have much of a plan."

Joe looked at her expressionless. "I'm kinda not surprised. 'Kay, let's hear what you wish could happen, and we'll figure out how we're actually gonna do this."

So the two came up with a plan, though it had a few holes, and they snuck around the machinery and headed toward the assembly room.

Hope and Joe stood just outside the assembly room, a cold draft from inside creeping through the crack in the open door.

"You ready for this?" Joe asked.

Hope's heart was beating faster than a hummingbird's, thumping against her chest so hard she swore it could break through. This was their only chance to make things better. If this failed ... that was it for them.

"I'm ready," she said, her voice more confident than she felt.

The two of them walked through the door, looking through the sea of small heads for one person in particular.

"God," Joe said. "They're ... they're babies."

Hope nodded, her eyes full of pain, as she continued searching.

She found Ben sifting through a box of metal parts propped on a bench, his small frame too short to reach the table.

"This way," Hope said, beckoning to Joe.

They hurried over to Ben, who looked up at Hope with his bright smile, his face smudged with grime.

"Hi, Miss Lady!" Ben said.

"Hello, Ben," Hope said. She managed her best attempt at a smile, her nerves twisting her stomach into a thousand knots.

"This is my friend, Joe. Joe works here. We need you to come with us, just for a moment. Are you okay with that?"

Ben looked around the room, presumably for an adult to tell him it was fine, but found no one.

"I'm not 'sposed to leave here, Miss Lady." Ben said, his voice a little quieter this time. "The mean guy comes in and yells in our faces.

"I promise he won't," Hope said, desperate to get the boy out. "How about I get you some sweets if you promise to come with us, just for a moment?"

When Ben's eyes lit up, she knew she had him. He stood up straight, stepping away from the box of metal parts, and then jumped up and down in excitement.

"Can I have all the sweets I want? Or do I only get one? My mama only lets me have one, but I always want lots more than that."

Hope grabbed his hand and led him out of the room as quickly and quietly as she could.

"I'll let you pick as many as you'd like, if this works out how we need it to," she said in a low voice.

Hope, Joe, and Ben hurried out of the assembly room and found the factory floor to be mostly free of prying eyes.

"We need to get to my father's office. Follow me," she said to Joe. Joe nodded, and trailed behind her as she ran down one of the aisles in the factory to the stairs at the other end. She constantly looked over her shoulder to make sure they weren't being followed. A few times, she caught Joe doing the same. They were only a few yards from the stairs. So very close. She looked behind her once more.

And she ran into what felt like a brick wall.

Hope stumbled back a bit, looking at what she had collided with. A cold chill ran up her spine, and her stomach roiled.

It was Tom, and he didn't just look angry. He looked... evil.

"And exactly where do you think you're going?" he said, his mouth curled in a sneer.

"Get outta the way," Joe said, stepping in front of Hope.

"Oh, you obnoxious little shadow of a man," Tom said, pushing Joe aside with ease. Joe stumbled to the side and fell over.

"You," he said, his eyes on Hope. "I told you to stay away. Looks like someone needs to be taught a lesson."

He grabbed Hope by the arm, his fingers digging into her arm to the point where Hope thought he'd break it.

"You're hurting me! Let go of me now!" she yelled. But her voice didn't carry very far over the buzzing sound of the machinery around them.

She frantically looked from side to side

for someone to call for, but with the reduced workforce, and the stairs being just far enough away from the main factory floor, there was no one to call to. Tom began dragging her past the stairs and away from Joe and Ben. She saw Joe get up from the ground ready for a fight. He couldn't overpower Tom, she thought. She couldn't either.

Their plan was failing miserably.

So she did the one thing she knew would get someone's attention. At least someone that'd get them away from whatever Tom had in mind.

Hope took a deep breath and screamed at the top of her lungs.

The sound vibrated in her ears and echoed off the walls and high ceiling of the factory. It carried to the edges of the building and, she could have sworn, shook the windows that lined the top of the factory walls.

All work in the factory ceased. Young eyes, old eyes, and eyes in between stared at them as Tom let go of Hope's arm and stumbled back.

She heard a thundering of feet above them, shoes clambering down the stairs and to the location of the shrill scream.

"What in the world was that?" came a voice.

Hope let out sigh of relief at the familiar voice.

Her father ran over to where she stood, Tom's face a mix of anger and, she was pretty sure, panic.

"Hope! What are you doing here? Did you not listen to a word I said?"

"I did, and I decided what's going on in this place is much more important than the threat of going to live with Aunt Muriel."

She looked over at Ben, who stood next to Joe. Ben's eyes were wide and fearful, his hands busying themselves with ringing his grubby little shirt. He scurried behind Joe, peeking at them from Joe's right side.

"Ben, come over here. Don't be afraid. You're safe, I promise," Hope said.

Ben's face disappeared behind Joe, and Joe gave him a reassuring pat.

"Go ahead," he muttered to Ben. "They ain't gonna hurt you."

Ben's gaze was pointed at the floor as he shuffled his torn up shoes over to where Hope stood. Hope held her hand out for him to grab. He looked at it suspiciously, then placed his hand in hers.

"This is Ben," Hope said to her father. "Ben, this is Mr. Patrick Richardson. He owns this factory, and he's also my father."

"You're Miss Lady's father?" Ben asked. He wiped his nose with the back of his hand, leaving a trail of dirt underneath his nose.

"Hello, Ben. What are you doing in my factory?" said Hope's father.

"I found him, along with a passel of other children about his age, working in the assembly room. Ben, why don't you tell Mr. Richardson how old you are."

Ben smiled a gap-toothed grin and held up all five fingers on his left hand.

"My God," her father said, stepping backward and bracing himself against the railing on the staircase.

"This is what's been going on in your factory when you let people like him make your decisions for you," Hope said, pointing at Tom.

Everyone's eyes shifted to Tom, who finally walked forward, shoulders set back in righteous indignation.

"I made the decisions that needed to be made, you little twit," he hissed, his eyes narrowing in Hope's direction.

"You, Mr. Peters," Hope's father said, standing in between Hope and Tom, "will never, ever speak to my daughter like that again. Watch your tone, old man."

"He threatened to fire Joe if I told you what's been happening here," Hope said as she motioned to Joe. "I found the children a week ago. You probably haven't heard much about them, because they've been cooped up in the assembly room this entire time."

Hope's father looked from Ben to Joe, then to Hope, then to Tom.

"I … I had no idea."

"Doesn't matter," Hope said. "This is your factory, and this is what happens when you want to be disconnected from things. You're still responsible."

Everything she'd felt over the past week– the inability to help at the factory, the sorrow she felt for the children working there, being made to feel like a useless fool by her father– all of it began to wash over her and pour into her words. She was angry.

"This," Hope continued, pointing to Ben, "this hiring of little children to do the work of men, is disgusting. It needs to end today. So you do what you have to do to make it right."

Joe's head jerked back in surprise at the tone she'd taken with her father. As the owner of the factory, no one spoke to him like that. But as his daughter, well, the closest he could get to firing her was to send her to Aunt Muriel, and she just didn't care anymore.

"You're right," he said.

Now it was Hope's turn to be shocked. She tilted her head to the side in confusion, definitely not expecting her father to see her side of things so quickly.

"This," he said, looking at Tom but pointing an open hand in Ben's direction, "is unacceptable. When I told you to 'make it work' I didn't mean hire children barely out of diapers. This is deplorable, Tom. And you—you may pack your things and leave immediately."

Tom walked toward her father, hands outstretched in surrender. "Now wait just a moment, Patrick ..."

"It's Mr. Richardson, and get out before I send for the police. You are now trespassing on private property."

Tom looked at Hope with narrowed eyes, probably wishing all sorts of awful things on her. But she simply smiled back with the satisfaction that he was now powerless and, well, jobless.

"Your factory is on its way to becoming a joke. Just you watch. This place is a success because of me."

"This," Hope's father said, gesturing to the half-empty factory behind them, "is not what I call a success. Now for the last time, get out."

Tom grumbled inaudibly as he returned to his office to gather his things. Tom called to one of the few men still working in the factory.

"Michael, my dear man, can you please see to it that Tom packs his things and leaves directly after?"

The man nodded, and her father gave him an appreciative pat on the back as the man walked toward Tom's office.

"Hope, I owe you an apology," her father said. "I'm sorry for what I said that day about you not being useful around here. You're extremely important to this place, and I'll make sure that you have as large a role here as you want."

"Forgiven," she said, grinning ear to ear. "And I accept."

"I've been a little too far behind the scenes of the day to day, and it's my own fault. Starting today, we turn over a new leaf. Sound good?"

Hope didn't think her grin could grow any wider, but it did. She looked over at Joe, who still stood a few feet away.

"Father, this is Joe. He's been fixing your machinery here at the factory. He almost lost his job helping me today, but he helped anyway."

"Well, my boy, I think I owe you my thanks. Thank you for helping my daughter today, and thank you for believing in her, even when I had foolishly stopped."

"Welcome, sir," he mumbled, ducking his head.

"Joe, did you just try to curtsy?" Hope laughed.

"No," he said defensively. "Think my knee gave out or something."

Hope's father laughed as well, and he even gave a curtsy of his own. "The pleasure, my boy, is all mine."

Things had a long way to go at the factory. The workers were still on strike, and there were plenty of negotiations that needed to happen before they were to resume. The children were to be sent home, but some kind of arrangements needed to be made with the families to ensure they still had a reliable income. Otherwise, they were helping no one by letting the children go.

But Hope had complete faith in her father. He had built his company up from nothing into something great, and she had no doubt that he could bring it back in no time.

Epilogue

It had been one month since Patrick Richardson took charge of his factory once again, and things had already taken a dramatic turn for the better. He sat with the striking workers, heard their grievances, and even listened to some of their suggestions.

One man in particular had a suggestion that would help cut costs, leaving more money to pay workers a fair wage. Hope's father had come home that night more excited than she'd ever seen him.

"Hope! You'd never believe it! It's a genius idea," he'd said. "We've been discarding any watch parts that aren't absolutely perfect. But if some of the pieces are good, just not completely perfect, they still make fine watch parts. So we use all those pieces and sell good watches for less than the original Richardson

Timepieces."

Hope had smiled at him, clapping her hands together. "And now more people can own watches, since they're not all so expensive anymore."

"Precisely," he'd said.

With the extra profit that was expected to come in from the pieces that would have otherwise been discarded, her father was able to minimize costs of watchmaking enough to grant the workers the wage they requested.

Many of the workers who had gone on strike had eventually sought employment elsewhere because of the length of the strike. To replace some of the lost workforce, he approached the families of the young children who had worked in the factory and offered a job with a fair wage to anyone old enough to work. And many of them took him up on his offer, allowing them to provide for their family and keep their children out of work.

As for Hope, well, Hope didn't know what the future held for her. She promised her father that she'd continue on with her lessons and not be so hard on her tutor. He said, "A lesson in conversation can just as easily be about entertaining your husband's colleagues as it could be about entertaining your own. So learn what you can, and make it yours."

So after a thrilling lesson in dancing (business could be conducted during a waltz, right?), she made the same walk she'd made so many times over to her father's factory. She walked straight through the lobby and onto the factory floor, passing machine after machine as she made her way to her destination.

The door to the assembly room was open, no longer hiding a dirty secret. She peeked in the doorway in search of someone in particular and waved when she'd found him.

Joe waved back and ambled across the room to meet her.

"How's it going, boss?" she asked.

"They're workin' hard. Can't complain about this group," he said.

Joe kept his supervisory role but had moved to the assembly room. Her father thought it could be problematic if the workers returned to their jobs to find a fourteen year old as their boss, yet Joe didn't deserve a demotion. So he took many of the younger employees who were still old enough to work and moved them to the assembly room. And Joe watched over them all. He did it well.

"Got about five minutes before this bunch goes on break," he said, looking down at his pocket watch.

"Well aren't you fancy?" Hope teased. "That's quite the nice timepiece you have there. Would that happen to be a Richardson pocket watch?"

"Is indeed. One of them new ones. Your pops gave it to me as a gift. Sharp, isn't it?"

Hope nodded in agreement. Joe looked happy in his new job, proud even. He'd taken a much different route than her in life, brought up in a very different life, but he seemed happy in it. She supposed that was more important than anything.

"Want to meet me when you're on your break?" she asked. "I'll wait around in the lobby."

"You got it."

Hope walked over to the lobby, and Joe joined her there a few minutes later.

"So what's next for you?" Joe said, taking a bite of his sandwich.

Hope looked out ahead as she thought about his question. She'd given it a lot of thought these past weeks.

"I suppose I could take over Richardson Timepieces one day. Though sometimes, well—" she said, trailing off at the end.

"Yeah? Sometimes what?"

"Sometimes I wonder if that's where I want to be. Or if it's something I wanted only because others said I couldn't have it, you know?"

Joe shrugged his shoulders and took another bite of his sandwich. He chewed voraciously, as if his sandwich were going to disappear if he didn't hurry to his next bite.

"So what else then?" he said.

"Well, those children—you know, the ones who worked here?"

Joe nodded, leaning forward to rest his arms on his knees, his half-eaten sandwich dangling from one hand.

"I wonder if there are other children like them. You know, children who are working in factories. Do you think I'd be able to help them?"

"Hope, I know you think I helped you last month. Takin' that boy Ben up to your dad or something. But that wasn't me. That was all you. So if that made you feel good, then you should keep doin' it. Right?"

Hope smiled and nodded. It was a dream, an inkling of an idea, that she'd had in the back of her mind for the past month, and today was the first she'd ever mentioned it aloud.

"You're right, Joe. You're pretty smart, did I ever tell you that?"

"I tell myself that every day," he said, his mouth full of food.

"My father's not going to be pleased."

"Maybe," Joe said. "But that never stopped you before."

Hope popped up from the bench they shared and clambered up the steps to the hallway leading to his office. She found her father at his desk, hunched over a large book that sat open on his desk.

"Hope! Come in, come in," he said. "To what do I owe this pleasure?"

Hope stood up straight and gave him her most sincere smile.

"Well, Father, I have the most wonderful idea. And I think you just might hate it."

About the Industrial Revolution

The Industrial Revolution has been considered one of the most important developments in human history since plants and animals were domesticated. It changed virtually every aspect of people's lives and caused dramatic growth in both population and per capita income.

The Industrial Revolution began in the United Kingdom, later spreading to the United States. The U.S. contributed a way to create interchangeable parts in machines, which was a major factor in it becoming the leading industrial nation by the late 1800s. Factories were originally powered by water, limiting production to cities with strong rivers, but the development of steam power allowed industry to spread to cities throughout the country.

J.D. Rockefeller was one of the most well-known and most-vilified figures from the Industrial Revolution. He helped found Standard Oil, the largest oil refinery of its time and became the richest man in the world through sometimes ruthless business practices. At one point, his own personal wealth made up 1.5 percent of the entire U.S. economy.

The Industrial Revolution had its ugly sides, though. Factory workers saw long hours, working anywhere from 10-12 hours every day and barely making enough money to support their families. The eventual development of unions helped protect workers from certain unfair labor practices, with workers striking when needs were not met. Children were often hired to work in factories, as factory owners could pay them a lower wage, and they were less likely to strike.

Q & A
with Brittany Canasi

1. Why did you choose to write a story from Hope's perspective?

Hope provided a unique perspective for this story. She was born into privilege but a prisoner because of it. Her struggle for a place in the world led her to help change things for better in the factory.

2. Why write about child labor?

The Industrial Revolution had a profound impact on Americans' daily lives. But there were some people who suffered as a result, and many of them were children. I felt it was an important story to tell.

About the Author

Brittany Canasi's job is in television, and her passion is in writing. She has a B.A. in Creative Writing from Florida State University. If she could be transported back to any time period, it would be England during the Regency era so that she could meet Jane Austen. She lives in Los Angeles with her husband and very scruffy dog, Dakota.

Websites to Visit

www.loc.gov/teachers/classroommaterials/
    lessons/child-labor
www.american-historama.org/industrial-
    revolution-inventions.htm
www.pbs.org/wnet/historyofus/web04/
    features/timeline.html

Writing Prompt

What invention from the Industrial Revolution do you find most interesting? Write a scenario in which it affects someone profoundly.